For Charly and Sam J.G.
For Sue, Patrick, Michael, Dominic and Tiziana J.B-B.

Text copyright © 2008 John Goodwin
Illustrations copyright © 2008 John Bendall-Brunello
This edition copyright © 2008 Lion Hudson

The moral rights of the author and illustrator
have been asserted

A Lion Children's Book
an imprint of
Lion Hudson plc
Wilkinson House, Jordan Hill Road,
Oxford OX2 8DR, England
www.lionhudson.com
ISBN 978 0 7459 6084 5

First edition 2008
1 3 5 7 9 10 8 6 4 2 0

A catalogue record for this book is available
from the British Library

Typeset in 18/24 Lapidary 333 BT
Printed and bound in China

The recording on the CD was produced and narrated by Bruce Pont for the ICC Media Group.
The Five-Minute Animal Stories music theme was composed and recorded by Bruce Pont for the ICC Media Group.

The stories on the CD have sounds denoting page turns to help the reader follow the text in the book.
The start and end of each story is denoted by the music theme.

The Lion Book of

Five-Minute
Animal Stories

Told by John Goodwin
Illustrated by John Bendall-Brunello

LION
CHILDREN'S

Contents

The Musicians of Bremen   6

Party Time   11

The Nightingale   16

The Cheeky Monkey   20

The Lion and the Mouse   23

Princess Petunia and the Pig   28

The Hare and the Hedgehog   32

Fish Girl   36

The Talking Bear   40

Chauntecleer the Cockerel   44

The Musicians of Bremen

A runaway donkey leads a dog, a cat and a horse to freedom in the town of Bremen. On the journey there they all learn something about friendship and out-of-tune singing.

EY NONNY no. Hee-haw noooooo!' sang the donkey in full voice. He'd never sung so happily in all his life. His master used to hate his singing. In fact, he stopped him from doing anything that looked even a little bit as if he was enjoying himself.

'I've run away from him and his cruelty to be freeeee!' hee-hawed the donkey. Over the hill, down the dale, along the river bank and through the woods he skipped and trotted.

His merriment was cut short as he heard a rustling in a hedge close by.

'I hope it's not my evil master coming to capture meee,' he brayed.

As he looked closer into the hedge, he saw a very thin dog trembling with fear.

'What's that terrible thunder?' cried the dog.

'That's no thunder,' brayed the donkey. 'It's just me singing. I'm off to Bremen. It's a big town where my master won't be able to find me. There I'll be freeee.'

'Can I come with you?' asked the dog quietly. 'I'd love to taste the sweetness of freedom from my cruel master.'

So the two set off together, with the dog howling quietly and the donkey braying very loudly indeed.

They had only travelled a short distance when they came to a prowling cat who immediately put both paws up to her ears.

'What a horrible row,' cried the cat.

'That's no row,' brayed the donkey. 'We're going off to Bremen to be freeee and I'm going to be a singer.'

'You're so out of tune,' called the cat. 'I'd better come with you. With my help, you can become the purrrfect minstrel.'

So the three went off together. After a while, they heard a thundering of hooves heading towards them.

'A runaway horse,' brayed the donkey.

'Out of my way,' whinnied the horse.

'I've just escaped. My master treated me like a slave. I haven't eaten anything for days.'

'Join our merry crew,' brayed the donkey. 'We're runaways too and we're bound for Bremennnn.'

It was dark by the time they reached the outskirts of Bremen and ahead they could see the lights of a building.

'I hope it's a shelter for the night,' said the dog quietly. 'I'm so tired.'

But when they came close to the building, they could hear humans inside. Timidly they peered in through the windows.

'All this treasure,' called one voice.

'We're the best thieves ever,' cried another.

'Brilliant burglars,' shouted a third.

'Let's share it all out,' said the fourth.

'That's my master in there,' howled the dog.

'And mine... and mine,' shrieked a pitiful animal chorus. Only the donkey kept his cool.

'It's pitch black out here so we can keep hidden,' he said. 'We've got to scare them like they've never been scared before. Make them panic. On the count of three, make more noise than you've ever made before. Are you ready? One, two, threeee...'

The donkey brayed with all his might and the horse hammered her hooves loudly on the door and whinnied wildly. The dog howled horribly and the cat's miaow was surely purrrfect.

Cries of anguish came from inside the building.

'Help, help.'

'It's the police, come to catch us.'

'Mercy on us.'

The humans came lurching and running wildly out of the building. It was the moment the animals had been waiting for.

Hooves kicked, claws scratched, voices growled and catcalls filled the night.

The thief masters were never heard of or seen again.

The animals have made the shelter their home. The donkey enjoys a big bowl of thistle soup and sings merrily between spoonfuls. The horse beats out the rhythm of the song with the clacking of her hooves while the dog snuffles in contentment. Curled up on a cushion, the cat purrs quietly. All the animals are at peace in their joyful home.

Party Time

All the animals are together for a special talent show. The camel
is especially nervous. How can she overcome her shyness?

IN THE sandy clearing, everything was quiet. No creature stirred or moved a muscle. All eyes were on the seal, who had a giant puffball balanced on the end of her nose. The seal suddenly broke the silence with a loud bark. She flicked the ball high into the air and then caught it again on the same spot on her nose. A round of applause rang out from the great crowd of animals that had gathered around. The seal's act wasn't finished yet, however. Her flipper sent up a second giant puffball, even bigger than the first, to land perfectly on top of the original ball. As if that wasn't enough, the same trick was done with a third ball. The crowd was amazed. They whistled and shouted their appreciation.

Next it was the turn of the elephant, who entered the arena with his huge swinging trunk. He lifted up his head and began to trumpet a song.

After one complete chorus, he stopped and swung his trunk round and round again.

'He wants us all to join in,' chipped in the chipmunk.

And so they did. Even the sloth sang, almost energetically, spurred on by the elephant's triumphant trumpet.

By now, the sun was setting in the sky and the moon began to shine. It was perfect timing for the zebra's magic stripe show. She dodged cleverly in and out of the moonlight. When she was lit brightly, her stripes were dazzling — and when she was in the shadow, she disappeared completely.

'Ooo, aah, it's magical,' cooed the animals.

Next came the kangaroo's high jump competition. The snake had the lowest jump to clear and the kangaroo the highest. The cheetah chuntered that the kangaroos had cheated and set their bar far too low. 'They'll win easily.'

But the cheetah was mistaken, for the tiny flea jumped higher than any other animal and was awarded a special miniature medal.

With the clearing bathed in moonlight, it was time for the monkeys to do fast-moving and

action-packed acrobatics. They swung between the trees on ropes. Some leaped even higher off the ropes and were caught by monkeys hanging upside down on the trees. Below them, other monkeys wearing hats made out of flowers jigged and jived and jogged about. Others did cartwheels and stunning backwards flips.

All this time, the shy camel had been looking very worried indeed.

'I don't have a single trick to show,' she thought to herself. 'I'm no good at anything.'

At the end of the show, she was the only animal who hadn't performed an act.

'Come on, camel,' said the crocodile. 'Don't let us down.'

All eyes turned to the camel and she couldn't hide from their gaze. She started to shake with fear, and the shake turned into a wobble. To stop herself from wobbling over, she put her front leg out.

'It's a dance, a crazy camel dance,' shouted the skunk. 'Let's all join in. Put your front leg out.'

Legs, claws, hooves, arms, flippers, tentacles and wings were thrust forward.

The camel drew back her leg to gain further stability.

'Front leg in,' chuckled the cuckoo.

The camel looked up to see what was happening and began to enjoy herself.

'You shake it all about,' she cried. 'You do the Hippity Hoppity and you turn around. That's what the fun's about.'

The clearing was full of hopping, dancing and capering animals. Some fell over in giggles and some joined together to make a long dancing line which wound in and out of the trees.

'Well done, camel,' hooted the wise owl. 'Each one of us has our own special talent — and you've just discovered yours.'

The Nightingale

The nightingale's song is said to be the most beautiful in the whole world. This is a story about that song and how powerful it finally proves to be.

THERE ONCE was an emperor of China whose empire spread many thousands of miles in every direction. The emperor was curious to know what was the most magnificent thing in his empire. So he sent for his most important noblemen to give him the answer. Perhaps he expected them to tell him it was his marvellous palace made entirely of porcelain. Instead, one very old and wise noble said, 'It is the song of a nightingale, a bird that lives in your garden, Your Imperial Majesty.'

The emperor was amazed and demanded to hear this bird in his garden that evening. Once they were outside, they all heard a long, low noise.

'That must be the nightingale,' declared a young noble.

'No, that is a cow mooing,' said the old noble.

They took a few more steps and another sound filled the air.

'That surely is the nightingale,' announced a third noble.

'Oh no. It's a frog's croak,' said the old noble, beginning to tire.

At last, they came to the heart of the garden — and the nightingale sang. Its song had a magical haunting beauty and everyone agreed it was magnificent. The emperor commanded that the nightingale be brought to his room so that he could listen to its song every night. When this was done, the emperor was happier than he'd ever been.

One day, the emperor of Japan came to visit.

'I have heard you have a songbird,' he said. 'But it is not as fine as this invention.'

The Japanese emperor clapped his hands and one of his many servants stood before him with a golden chest. Inside the chest was a shiny mechanical toy that he wound up by hand. When the winding was complete, the toy sang out just like the nightingale. The young nobles were very impressed.

'It is perfect.'

'You can listen to the song all day and every night.'

'So much better than the plain brown bird.'

The mechanical bird became the most popular possession in the emperor's palace and the real nightingale was forgotten entirely.

One winter's morning, something terrible happened. Instead of singing the melodious song, the mechanical toy went *twang*. The winding-up part was broken and no one could mend it.

The emperor was heartbroken and became ill.

'Find me the real bird,' he decreed.

But alas, the real nightingale could not be found anywhere. As days turned to weeks, nobody could even remember what the nightingale's song sounded like.

'Was it a *warble wombat womble?*' asked one of the nobles.

'Or *wombat babble womble?*'

'Or *bobble babble bobble?*'

The emperor's health grew worse and everyone feared he might die. Each evening, the old nobleman searched the palace garden and spent hours waiting at the place where the nightingale had first appeared. Every night, the window in the emperor's bedroom was left slightly open with the hope that the bird would fly in. But all these efforts were in vain.

The emperor was so ill that the doctors said the window must be closed, for even a slight chill would kill their patient. However, the very weak emperor forbad them to do so.

One night, the moon was no more than a silver crescent in the sky. It was so dark in the palace garden that the old noble could barely see his hand in front of his face. When he felt something land on his hand, however, his heart gave a leap and he knew immediately what he must do. He carefully carried the small bird

to the open window of the emperor's bedroom.

Soon the nightingale began to sing. The emperor lay very still and listened to it once more in wonder. He whispered, 'What was lost is found. We only know true worth when it is taken away from us.'

As time passed, the nightingale came every night to sing to the emperor and his health returned.

The Cheeky Monkey

A greedy monkey doesn't learn after he makes a big mistake.

THE MONKEY enjoyed himself in the rajah's palace. He went out into the palace garden and picked bananas from the trees. Quicker than you could say the word 'banana', he would run up the banana tree, flick back the skins and stuff the yellow fruit into his mouth. Without taking a breath, he would do the same with a second banana and a third. Yet even with bulging cheeks, the monkey still felt hungry.

The monkey also liked to eat dates and apples and pears and cherries. Best of all were the days when the rajah had special feasts in the palace. Then he could do no wrong. The rajah would laugh at the monkey as he took mangoes and pomegranates from his own table and scurried off with them like a naughty thief.

One night after a big feast, the rajah was fast asleep in his bedroom. On his dressing table was his magnificent ruby. It was as big as your fist. It shone brighter than any star and it was redder

than any berry or fruit.

When the rajah woke up the next morning, he saw that his priceless jewel had disappeared.

'Search everywhere,' he shouted. 'Search all the servants. Someone has stolen it.'

The search went on all day but the ruby couldn't be found.

'I must have it back,' shouted the rajah. 'Search again. Someone must have hidden it.'

The whole palace was turned upside down again but the result was just the same.

Then someone noticed the monkey's bulging cheek. When he was taken to the rajah, the ruby was found stuffed in the monkey's mouth – for the greedy animal thought he could take anything of the rajah's.

'There is no place for thieves in my palace,' said the rajah. 'Take the animal far away and make sure it never returns.'

The monkey was taken to a different part of the country where there was very little fruit to eat. Here the ground was frozen and the sky was full of snow. The monkey swung from tree to tree longing for something to nibble on, but there was nothing. One day, he stopped. He was sure he could smell food. The monkey looked all around and spied a hole part way up a tree.

He ran up close to see what he could find. Inside was a hoard of nuts. He reached inside and it felt so good as he grabbed some.

However, the monkey's hand was just so full of nuts that he couldn't pull his fist out. Just then, a big red bird with a bright eye came by and cackled, 'You'll have to let some go.'

'I won't,' shouted the monkey angrily. 'I'm hungry and I want to eat them all.'

He pulled and he pulled.

He squeezed his fist tight shut and pulled again.

He took a deep breath and pulled even harder.

But his fist was stuck in the hole in the tree.

In the end, the monkey had to let all of the nuts go.

'I don't care,' he shouted. 'I didn't want the stupid nuts anyway.'

With both hands free, he swung through the forest looking for something else to eat. Then the squirrels came and each took a single nut from the store. The big bird simply cackled.

The Lion and the Mouse

When the lion saves the mouse's life, little does he realize how the kindness will be repaid.

THE LION was having a snooze in the warmth of the sun when he felt a tiny tickle on his nose. He tried to ignore it but the tickle grew into an itch. Without opening his eyes, the lion tried to waft the itch away with a lazy waft of his paw. That's when the itch grew to a twitch.

The lion opened his eye a smidgen to see that a mouse was crawling over his face.

'How dare you,' boomed the lion, grabbing the mouse in his giant paw.

'Please spare me, sir,' squeaked the trembling mouse.

'Huh,' grumbled the lion. 'You've woken me up. And I don't like anyone or anything that does that.'

'I meant no harm,' squeaked the mouse. 'Your face is so huge. I thought I was climbing up a steep mountain.'

'Stupid creature,' bellowed the lion. 'I'm going to eat you this very minute.'

The lion opened his mouth and the mouse looked into the massive black hole she was just about to be swallowed into. She let out such a shriek that the lion in surprise eased his grip on the mouse's body. The mouse quickly wriggled out of the paw and bounded free.

'Thank you, kind lion,' she squeaked. 'You're so generous to grant me freedom.'

But the lion was just as quick-thinking as the mouse and once more grabbed her tightly in his paws.

'Who said I was generous?' he bellowed in the mouse's ear.

'You are surely a very kind animal, and for that I'll make you a promise,' squeaked the mouse.

'What promise?'

'If you spare my life, I'll be sure to repay you with kindness,' squeaked the mouse very seriously indeed.

The lion let out a huge guffawing laugh. 'How could you ever keep such a promise?'

'Just save my life now and you'll see,' squeaked the mouse.

The lion didn't believe the promise would ever happen but he let the mouse scuttle away.

Time passed. The lion roamed the plains and waterholes and forgot about the mouse. But the lion was being watched. Men were tracking the king of creatures. They were hunters

determined to capture him for money.

One day, the lion was having his usual doze when something tickled his nose. This time it wasn't a mouse's tiny feet but a huge net that had been dropped over his body. By the time the lion realized what was happening, it was too late. He snarled and lashed out with his powerful claws. But the more he struggled, the more he became ensnared in the mesh of the net. Before too long, his strength was spent and he knew that it was impossible to escape the trap.

As night fell, the hunters saw his exhaustion and knew they had won. Early the next morning, they would transport the lion away in a cart and he would never see the jungle again. Or so they thought.

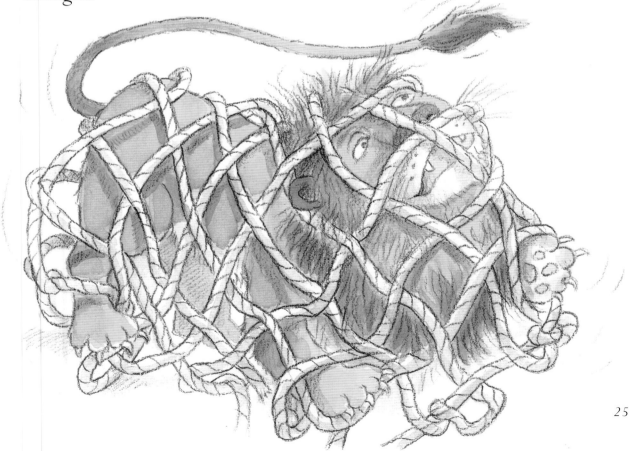

The lion heard something squeak close by.

'Don't move,' said the squeak.

'Who's there?' asked the lion.

'Your little friendly mouse, come to keep her promise.
Keep quite still. I'm going to set you free.'

'How can you do that?' asked the lion.

The mouse didn't answer for she was already at work on
the fibres of the net. Her teeth might be tiny but they were very
sharp and she had already cut through one strand of the fibre.

Nibble. Cut, nibble, scratch. Chomp, bite, gnaw. That's how
the mouse spent the night, and by first light the next morning
she was ready. She had cut just enough fibres to make a hole large
enough for the lion to creep through. The lion escaped the net
and the two of them sneaked off to safety, far away from
the hunters.

Princess Petunia and the Pig

Greedy Petunia soon finds herself in real trouble.

PRINCESS PETUNIA loved her food. For breakfast she ate a queen-sized bowl of porridge and cream, two eggs and three cakes, and she drank five golden goblets of quince juice.

Sometimes her skinny mother, Queen Esmerelda, would say, 'Petunia darling, don't be a pig. You're not having any trifles today and that's final.'

That meant trouble of the very BIGGEST kind. Petunia stamped her feet, pulled her hair and ripped the bows and ribbons off her dress. But worse of all, she SHOUTED VERY LOUD until her mother gave in.

It was Princess Petunia's birthday. That meant there would be a royal banquet in her honour. It was Petunia's chance to eat even more than usual.

Before the eating came the dressing up. Petunia had a sparkling new dress to wear. They tried to pull it over her head but Petunia squealed. They tried to lift it over her feet but Petunia kicked it off. They tried to push it over her arms but Petunia lashed out with her fists. The dress was too small and Petunia was too fat.

King Ernie, her father, had a stern talk to her.

'Don't stuff yourself with food tonight, Petunia,' he said. 'Just eat sensibly.'

But Petunia would have none of it and she ate and ate and ate. She'd just tucked into the biggest meringue in the world when she began to feel rather strange. Her skin began to itch and her ears began to grow. Then her fingers and toes turned into trotters and her nose grew HUGE. Petunia had turned into a pig.

She tried to speak but the only sound that came out of her mouth was a grunt. Someone placed a collar round her neck and she was led away to the nearest field. There was no warm bed for her to lie in now – only black mud and a wooden fence to keep her from escaping.

Petunia had to stay in the field all night and most of the next morning. Around lunchtime, she saw her father's golden coach out on the road next to the field. She ran across to the coach as quickly as her trotters would carry her.

'Help me, please,' she cried, but her father only laughed at her grunts.

'Don't you recognize me?' she called. 'I'm Petunia.'

'Drive on, coachman,' shouted her father. 'It's time for lunch.'

Petunia stared hard at the disappearing coach. 'Time for lunch,' he'd said. Usually she'd be ravenous at this time of day but today she wasn't the least bit hungry. As the days passed, she ate a few acorns but nothing else.

Early one morning, Petunia looked at her reflection in the stream. 'I've lost weight,' she grunted.

She ran across to the fence which enclosed the whole field and looked closely at the gap between the fence poles. Surely she could squeeze herself through that gap? She pushed her snout into the gap and she pushed and squeezed and wriggled.

The next moment, she was through the fence and heading off towards the royal palace. The further she went, the more her trotters felt like human legs. The more she sniffed the warm spring air, the more it felt like she had a nose and not a snout.

'Please let me be human again,' she cried. 'I'll never pig out on my food again. And I'll try not to be selfish or rude.'

When she had returned to a human, Petunia kept her promise. She still had a weakness for the occasional meringue but her dress size grew smaller and she was the model of good behaviour.

The Hare and the Hedgehog

The hedgehog's cunning plan turns sour in a clumsy fall.

IT WAS a fine sunny day when the hare met the hedgehog. The hare was combing his fur with the help of a teasel that was growing in the hedgerow.

'My fur is sleek and beautiful,' boasted the hare. 'I can run faster than the wind. Just look how I can leap and jump and do somersaults high in the air.'

After the hare showed off all his tricks, the hedgehog said quietly, 'How would you like a race, then?'

'A race with you?' sneered the hare.

'Down the length of this long field,' said the hedgehog. 'The loser will give the winner a bottle of forest fruits fizz.'

The hare could not believe his luck and the two shook paws on the challenge without delay.

'We'll start straight away,' said the hare, doing warm-up press-ups on a clover patch.

'Oh no. I'm going home to have a little snooze first,' mumbled the hedgehog as her stumpy little feet disappeared through the gate of the field.

When the hedgehog arrived home and explained the bet to her husband, he became very angry.

'You must be crazy. Hedgehogs just don't do racing.'

He hated the thought of giving away one of his prize bottles of blackberry fizz, especially to the show-off hare.

'You're bound to lose,' he moaned.

'Not with my cunning plan,' said his wife.

'What cunning plan?'

'We two look exactly alike, don't we?' said Mrs Hedgehog.

Mr Hedgehog agreed that they did.

'The corn has been cut in the field except for a strip down the middle,' continued his wife. 'You make your way to the finishing line of the race between the stalks without the hare seeing you. I'll start the race in the same row of stalks and then disappear from view. All you have to do is come out at the bottom of the stalk row. You stagger over the finishing line just before the hare and we've won.'

'So you start the race and I finish it,' said Mr Hedgehog.

'Exactly,' said Mrs Hedgehog. 'The hare will never know there are two of us.'

'It will never work,' said Mr Hedgehog.

'Of course it will. Hares can run fast but they have no brains.'

So the race began. The hare went off in a fast sprint but Mrs Hedgehog had barely moved. Soon the hare was near the finishing line and Mrs Hedgehog was far behind and out of sight.

'This is easy,' said the hare to himself. 'Easy peasy.' He made a great leap in the air. 'I'll win that forest fruits fizz for sure.'

Something was moving slowly ahead of the hare. Something prickly with a very pointy nose had crossed the finishing line first and won the race.

'I don't believe it,' grumbled the hare. 'How did you do that?'

Mr Hedgehog shrugged his prickles.

'It's just skill,'
he said modestly.
'We'll rerun the race and this
time I'm bound to win,' shouted the hare.
So they ran the race again and the hedgehogs
played the same trick. They repeated the race 63 times
until the hare was worn out, and each time the hedgehogs won.
The hedgehogs carried off their prize in glee, congratulating
themselves on their cleverness. But they had cheated, and cheats
never prosper; and sure enough, just before they reached home,
the bottle of forest fruits fizz slipped from their grasp and
smashed on a stone on the ground. 'There's not a drop left to
drink,' moaned Mr Hedgehog, and they were both miserable for
days afterwards.

Fish Girl

Lotkia is more fish than human but finds her own happiness eventually.

LOTKIA HAS the deepest blue eyes you could ever see and a web of skin that grows between her fingers and toes. Most of the time, she sits and looks out to sea in the small fishing village where she lives with her mother and father.

'Don't just sit there, girl,' grumbles her father. 'We need you to help around the home. Why are you so lazy?'

Lotkia doesn't answer. She only has thoughts for the deep blue ocean.

There are many small children in the village who spend their time playing games and having fun.

'Fly a kite with me, Lotkia,' they call.

'Join in the ball game with us.'

'Run a race, Lotkia.'

But Lotkia will have none of it and she makes no friends at all. In time, the children lose patience with her and call her names.

'Moody girl.'

'Fish face.'

One sunny day, Lotkia's mother takes her down to the sea to cheer her up.

'I'll teach you to swim,' she says.

As Lotkia looks at the white foaming waves breaking on the seashore, her face breaks into a giant smile. Before her mother can stop her, Lotkia is jumping through the waves. She swims like she's made for the sea and needs no teaching.

From that time on, there is only one place that Lotkia wants to be. Come rain or sun, wind or storm, it's the beach for her. Soon she swims with the dolphins way out in the bay.

'Not so far out, Lotkia,' calls her mother. 'It's too dangerous out there. You're too far from the beach.'

But her daughter only has ears for the cries and calls of the dolphins and she doesn't want to hear her mother at all.

One day when Lotkia goes swimming by herself, the dolphins call to her, 'Swim away with us. Come far away to the magic of the ocean.'

That was the day Lotkia disappeared and didn't come home. Though her mother and father search long and hard, they don't find her. Months pass and there is still no sign of the girl. On a windy day, a small fishing boat comes into the harbour and begins to haul up its net.

'It's a heavy catch,' says a fisherman.

'Mostly seaweed,' says a second fisherman.

But when the captain looks into the net, he sees something very strange indeed and immediately sets off in the direction of Lotkia's parents' cottage.

When her parents come to the boat, they know they've found their daughter. As they hug her, they see how changed she is. Her skin is scaly and she's now more fish than human.

When they take Lotkia home, her father is determined to lock her in the house. 'Bolt the door. She won't escape a second time.'

As the wind grows into a full-force storm, her mother hugs her closely. She looks down into Lotkia's deep blue eyes and sees a great haunting beauty in them. When the lightning flashes, the sheen on Lotkia's body turns into a thousand glistening rainbow colours.

'Open the door,' she says to her husband. 'We have to let her go to her own water world. It's where she wants to be.'

And so Lotkia is taken to the water's edge and her deep sea home. Most days, father and mother see their daughter when she swims to the surface. They smile and wave from the shore and are happy that their daughter has found contentment in her own new world.

The Talking Bear

The bear's love of honey leads him into clever tricks.

THE BIG brown bear liked honey better than anything else in all the world. He loved to find a honeycomb and lick the sticky yellow sweetness of honey from his paws. What he didn't like were bees around the honeycomb. Bees stung him on the nose and buzzed in his ear.

So the bear went off to look for honey somewhere else. He went to the mountains. Human travellers came up there to walk and climb the mountain peaks. The humans carried rucksacks that had juicy honey sandwiches in them.

The crafty bear would wait for the travellers to sit down for a rest. Once they took their rucksacks off their backs, he would sneak up on them. Then he would suddenly show himself, growl very loudly and wait for the travellers to run off in panic. The plan never failed. Sometimes the bear would find jam instead of honey in the sandwiches but he didn't mind that too much.

The bear learned to play tricks on the humans. Sometimes they would have a quick nap once they had taken off their rucksacks. Then the bear would pinch their sandwiches without them knowing. When they woke up, they would say to each other, 'Have you eaten all the sandwiches?'

'No, I haven't eaten any.'

'You must have done, because there are none here. You ate them while I was asleep.'

'I tell you — I haven't touched them!'

Then the humans would argue. The bear loved that. He would hide behind a tree or rock listening to them. That's how he taught himself to speak human. At first, he could only make a few human sounds. After a while, the sounds turned to words. With more practice, he began to speak whole sentences.

One day, the bear was on a stony and steep path that led up to the tallest mountain. He heard human voices below.

'We've come far enough,' said one.

'It's not far to the top,' said the second. 'Let's go on further.'

The bear came down the track for a closer look at the two travellers.

One – who was very red in the face – was mopping his head with a handkerchief. The second looked very fit and was checking his map.

Both had bulging rucksacks on their backs.

'Time for fun!' thought the bear as he sneaked up on them. When he was really close, he launched himself onto the path. Both humans turned to see a huge bear. They stared in horror at the sharpness of the bear's teeth and the power of his claws. In a scream of panic, the red-faced one began to run away. Fortunately, a small tree was growing by the path and he climbed up to the top.

The fit-looking one was left to face the danger alone. The bear growled loudly. Then he began to advance, taking one giant footstep after another. The fit one could feel his heart pounding in his body.

'I know, I'll pretend to be dead,' he said to himself and he let himself fall down straight to the ground where he lay very still. The bear came closer and sniffed his body. Then he licked his face, whispered something in his ear and climbed off back up the track.

When the red-faced one was sure the bear had gone for good, he climbed down the tree.

'What did the bear whisper?' he asked the fit-looking one.

'He gave me this advice,' said the fit-looking one: 'Never travel with a friend who deserts you in a time of danger. Real friends will stand by you through thick and thin.'

Chauntecleer the Cockerel

A cockerel lets himself be deceived by clever words from a cunning fox.

DOWN AMONG the cabbages, a fox is lurking. Her ginger body moves stealthily towards a cluster of hens that are feeding in the orchard.

'Cluck,' cries a hen.

'Cluck, cluck,' calls a second.

'Cluck, cluck, cluck,' clucks a third.

Even though they can't see the fox, the hens sense the danger and they scurry off out of the orchard.

Chauntecleer the cockerel ignores them. He is oblivious to any danger and proudly struts about in his brightly coloured feathers. The fox is so close to Chauntecleer that she can almost snap him up with her very sharp teeth. Almost but not quite.

The fox is crafty and decides to set a trap with some carefully chosen words.

'What beautiful feathers you have, Chauntecleer,' says the fox

in a very smarmy voice. 'They are brighter than the sun.'

'Thank you, kind fox,' replies Chauntecleer. 'They are indeed beautiful.'

'I have heard you have something even finer than your feathers,' says the fox. 'Something that makes you world famous.'

'World famous, eh?' says Chauntecleer, fluffing up his feathers.

'Oh yes,' says the fox. 'Everyone speaks of your amazingly brilliant cock-a-doodle-do and I'd very much like to hear it.'

'And so you shall,' says Chauntecleer.

Chauntecleer clears his throat with a very tiny cluck. Then he thrusts his golden neck out and his wings back. Everything is ready for the cock-a-doodle-do of the century. Chauntecleer closes one eye and lets rip.

'Cock-a-doodle-do,' rings out into the morning air clearer than a bell.

The crafty fox waits for a second before saying, 'That is perfect. Truly amazing. I can see why you are so famous.'

'Thank you,' says the cockerel before strutting about.

'It was so dazzling that I'd love to hear it again,' says the fox.

Chauntecleer prepares himself again and closes both eyes this time.

The fox pounces and grabs the cockerel between her jaws. Then she runs off with Chauntecleer out of the orchard.

The hens see what's happening and cluck loudly.

The cats miaow because the hens cluck.

The cows moo because the cats miaow.

The dogs bark because the cows moo.

Farmer Bessie runs out of the farmhouse because the dogs bark and she falls over a bucket in the farmyard.

She cries out.

Her children run out of the barn when they hear her cry out.

And the whole farm is in uproar.

Everyone runs after the fox.

'Stop, stop,' they all call.

But the fox runs faster than any of them.

It looks like nothing can save poor Chauntecleer.

But…

Chauntecleer has one last plan to try. It had already been tried once that day and it succeeded. Could it win through a second time?

'You are a clever animal,' says Chauntecleer, trying not to snag his body on the fox's teeth.

The fox grunts in agreement through clenched jaws.

'Your cunning has beaten us all,' says Chauntecleer.

Again the fox grunts.

'You should shout out your triumph and let everyone know how victorious you are,' says the cockerel.

The fox opens her mouth very wide to call out. The cockerel flies out of the fox's open jaws and escapes to safety.

'Phew,' says Chauntecleer, breathing easier.

'If you weren't so vain, it wouldn't have happened,' clucks one of the hens.

'Foxes and cockerels are both vain,' moos the cow. 'It's only us cows that are sensible animals. We may be boring – eating grass all day – but at least we don't let ourselves be fooled by smarmy words.'

Down in the orchard Chauntecleer walks around slowly, still very shaken after his ordeal.